Fanny Blake was a publisher for many years, editing both fiction and non-fiction before becoming a freelance journalist and writer. She has written various non-fiction titles, acted as ghost writer for a number of celebrities, and is also Books Editor of Woman & Home magazine. To find out more visit www.facebook.com/FannyBlakeBooks or follow her on Twitter @FannyBlake1

### By Fanny Blake

What Women Want
Women of a Dangerous Age
The Secrets Women Keep
With a Friend Like You

# Red for Revenge

## Fanny Blake

An Orion paperback

First published in Great Britain in 2015
by Orion Books
an imprint of The Orion Publishing Group Ltd,
Orion House, 5 Upper St Martin's Lane,
London WC2H 9EA

An Hachette UK company

1 3 5 7 9 10 8 6 4 2

A CIP catalogue record for this book
is available from the British Library.

ISBN 978 1 4091 5746 5

Typeset at The Spartan Press Ltd,
Lymington, Hants

Printed in Great Britain by CPI Group (UK) Ltd,
Croydon, CR0 4YY

The Orion Publishing Group's policy is to use papers that
are natural, renewable and recyclable products and made
from wood grown in sustainable forests. The logging and
manufacturing processes are expected to conform to the
environmental regulations of the country of origin.

www.orionbooks.co.uk

# Red for Revenge

# Chapter One

Maggie Blackburn looked up as another customer entered the otherwise empty nail bar. The
woman had come up from the treatment rooms
in the basement. Maggie's first instinct was to
tidy her hair but that was impossible. Both her
hands were dipped in nail soakers. If she had
known that a facial would leave her looking as
if she had been dragged through a hedge, she
would never have had one. She didn't feel right
facing the world with her hair all oily and on
end. As soon as she could escape to go home and
have a shower, the better she would feel.

Phil, her husband, had given her the gift
voucher to Beauty Unlimited as a Christmas
present. 'Treat yourself,' he had said, although
she knew he didn't really expect her to. Worse,
she suspected he didn't really care whether she
did or not. However, she wanted to look her best
for their anniversary dinner that evening.

Phil had promised he would be home on time
for once. He often stayed late at work these
days. He was working extra hard to earn the

1

promotion he so badly wanted, so she didn't like to complain. Instead, she had persuaded him to book a table at the new Italian restaurant on the High Street. This would be the first time they had gone out together for ages. She was determined to make the evening a success.

The new customer was shown to the seat beside Maggie's. She sat down with a relieved 'Oof.' Smiling at Maggie, she straightened the skirt of her dress. 'I shouldn't groan like that. It makes me sound so old.' She studied Maggie for a moment. 'Just had a facial? Plays havoc with your hair, doesn't it? I always go for the full body massage.'

'I've never had one before. I didn't know.' Maggie said. The idea of her plump neighbour lying naked on a massage bed struck her with some horror. Maggie would never remove her own clothes in front of a stranger. And she certainly wouldn't have them touch her all over.

She had chosen the facial because it was the least embarrassing option. But now she was embarrassed that the state of her hair had been noticed. She gave her hand to the girl who was waiting to treat her nails. She was struck by the contrast between her own skin and the girl's smooth tanned arm. The word 'STRIDENT' was tattooed on it.

'Really! Never?' The other woman sounded surprised. She was studying the nail varnish samples. 'I treat myself to a massage whenever I can afford it. Makes all the difference. You should try it.'

Maggie studied her neighbour. She had a round, rather pretty face, friendly eyes and a wide smile. Her shiny brown hair lapped the collar of her mauve dress which was slightly too tight. On her feet was a pair of deep violet suede heels. Did other women really dress like this every day, and not just at parties?

'Gorgeous aren't they?' The woman lifted one foot and turned it in a circle. 'I couldn't resist.'

'Mmm. I'd love to wear something like that.' Maggie remembered her own wardrobe – dull, some might say – and looked at the shoes with envy.

'Why don't you, then?' The woman held the varnish samples against her fingers one after the other, as she searched among the pale pinks and neutrals for the right colour. 'You only live once, so you might as well choose the shoes you like. We'll all be in those awful "natural" things and hanging on to Zimmer frames before we know where we are.'

Maggie laughed, warming to the woman. 'Don't! But I'd feel too self-conscious.'

'Nonsense. Don't worry about what other people think. You've got to dress for yourself.' She pointed to a soft peachy pink. 'Nude Peach. That's the one.'

Maggie looked over. 'That's the same one I've chosen.' Not the colour she would have imagined this larger-than-life woman would choose at all. She would have expected her to go for something much more brazen.

'Really?' The woman held out her hand so that the other manicurist could work on her nails. 'To be honest, if it was up to me, I'd have one of those – Strawberry Crush or Ruby Rose. But my boyfriend hates them. He thinks they're tarty.'

'So you do care what he thinks.' Maggie winced as the manicurist clipped at her cuticles.

'Well, of course I want him to appreciate me and if that's what it takes . . .' She gave Maggie a crafty smile. 'Well, it's not much is it? I'm Carla by the way. I'd shake hands if you weren't busy.' Her laugh reminded Maggie of a machine-gun. Rat-a-tat-tat.

'Maggie.' Maggie introduced herself, liking the instant rapport she felt with this woman. She rarely made new friends these days.

'My husband doesn't like those hot pinks or reds either.' Maggie looked at them. If only she had the nerve to try one of them. Classy Coral perhaps. But how the children would laugh at her. How her mother-in-law would look down her nose. Phil would do the same. 'Mutton dressed as lamb,' he'd say. Just as he had when she tried wearing a skirt that stopped a couple of inches above her knees. Once upon a time he had admired her legs.

'Men are funny,' Carla said. 'I don't know why we try so hard to please them, really. Makes life easier I suppose. Been married long?'

'Twenty-five years. Since we left school.' Even as she said it, Maggie felt weary. Twenty-five years and what had she got to show for it? Two children who had left home as soon as possible. A husband who barely seemed to notice her. These days, Phil never asked what she thought about anything or inquired how her day at work had been.

The twenty-five years had been spent looking after the family, doing housework or homework, and being polite to the school parents. As school secretary, she often had to cope with people who thought nothing of being rude to her.

'We only had ten years together.' Carla looked thoughtful.

Divorce was hard. Maggie had seen too many of her friends go through it. Besides, ten years wasn't that bad for a marriage. Maggie was about to sympathise but Carla went on.

'He was a builder. A breeze block fell off some flats where he was working and hit him square on the head. He was dead before he hit the ground. He was only thirty-five.' She sank back into her chair and sighed. For a second, the life seemed to go out of her.

There was a moment of silence only broken by the click of nail scissors. Outside a car horn hooted.

'Bloody waste,' Carla said, before appearing to regain her energy. 'But what can you do? Just got to pick yourself up and get on with life. You've only got one. That's what he taught me.'

'How dreadful.' Maggie didn't know what to say, especially since Carla didn't seem to be looking for sympathy. 'Did you have children?' she tried.

Carla roared with laughter. 'God no! We never got round to that. Too busy enjoying ourselves. The only sensible thing Ian did in his life was to buy us a flat. I had to sell it after he died though. I couldn't live there without him. So it's thanks to him that I've got my house now. It's small mind, but it's nice. And it's mine. So the poor sod did look after me – just not in the way he thought he would.' She gave a little shrug of her shoulders. 'Have you got children?'

'Two. But they've left home. Jack's married now.' Maggie thought of her tall, athletic son with a pinch of sadness. 'We hardly see him any more. He's too busy with the garage, and with Gail. She's his wife,' she added. They had moved to live near Gail's parents. Gail didn't want to share him with Maggie and Phil.

Maggie stopped herself. That wasn't fair. Gail was a nice girl really. She just wanted the best for her husband.

'And Kelly's just started studying nursing at uni in Swansea. She wants to be a midwife.' She said this with pride. Kelly was doing something with her life. That was exactly what Maggie wished she had done with her own. But instead, she and Phil had met at school, married as soon as they left and she fell pregnant soon after. She had gone from part-time job to part-time job for years – dinner lady, typist, hotel reception-ist – until Miss Fletcher, the head teacher of the local primary school, suggested she took a maternity cover for the school secretary. Mag-gie's somewhat rusty secretarial skills and love of organisation had helped a lot, and she was still there.

'And your husband? What does he do?' Carla

7

stretched her fingers in front of her as her manicurist turned to get the moisturiser.

'Phil? He's—'

The other woman glanced at her. 'Phil? How funny. That's my boyfriend's name.'

Maggie smiled. 'Well, there are plenty of them about. Mine works at Plums, the supermarket chain. Head office.' She didn't want her new friend to think he was a shelf stacker at their age. 'He's a buyer. Canned soups.'

How proud she had been when he first began to work there. He used to come home every night and regale her with stories of what had gone on during his day and she would listen, entranced, admiring. The problems began when she had nothing to tell him back. Nothing that interested him anyway. The routine of her days was dull to him. What happened at school or to the kids was nothing compared to the politics on the trading floor or higher up the chain of command.

'He's hoping for a promotion,' she added.

Maggie was surprised when Carla didn't respond. She stopped studying her nails, now shining with the first coat, and turned to her. 'And your boyfriend?' she prompted. 'What does your Phil do?'

Carla was looking down. Although her hair

had fallen across her face, Maggie could see that her face was flushed red. She sympathised. The menopause was hell to live with. She had had it early so she knew. She waited for a moment, knowing there was no point in rushing her new friend until the flush had died away. Then: 'Where does he work?'

'I, er...' Carla stopped.

Maggie waited, watching the care with which her manicurist worked, painting each nail so precisely. 'You haven't forgotten have you?' she joked.

'He, er...' Carla shook her head as if trying to clear it. 'Er, he works at Plums too.'

'Really?' Maggie sat back in her chair and admired her finished nails. Nice. She would come here again. 'How funny. Which department?'

'He's in, er...' The woman took a breath. 'He's a buyer too.'

'No! But they must know each other. I'll ask Phil tonight. We're going out to celebrate our anniversary. That's why...' She stopped. The same nail colour. The same name. The same company. And the woman she had befriended so easily looking as if she wished she were anywhere but in the next chair.

There was a rushing in Maggie's ears, a feeling of being lifted up and thrown down helpless in front of an express train that was thundering towards her.

This couldn't be happening...

Not again.

'What's his last name?' she forced herself to ask, not wanting to hear the answer. But at the same time knowing she had to.

'Blackburn.' Carla said the word so fast, Maggie almost didn't hear it. The other woman was staring straight in front of her as if willing the manicurist to finish her nails in double-quick time. But both the white-jacketed girls were still. They were listening to every word.

'Blackburn.' Maggie repeated. Perhaps she had misheard.

Carla nodded, then swallowed. 'I work there too – in pickles and sauces.'

'As a buyer?'

She nodded again. 'I'm sorry. He told me...'

But Maggie didn't want to listen to what her husband had told Carla. All she could feel was a terrible sense of shame. What an idiot, she had been. She had believed Phil when he said it would never happen again. She should have known better. Once a cheat... She pushed the table aside and stood up, waving her hands so her nails would dry faster.

'I'd like to pay.' She crossed to the till and

waited as the bill was printed, unable to speak. All she could do was concentrate on staying upright and breathing. In. Out. In. Out. Somehow she managed to fumble her gift voucher from her purse without smudging her nails. Funny how important that still seemed.

Maggie didn't listen to what the girl was saying to her. She ignored the shout of 'Wait!' from Carla. She only wanted to get out of there and get home. Phil had promised her. He had promised.

A bell tinkled as she opened the door, and again as she slammed it behind her. In the street, the cold air felt good on her burning cheeks. But nothing could clear the red cloud of hurt and anger that raged inside her head. She leaned against the wall, feeling its chill through her jacket, and closed her eyes. The bastard!

# Chapter Two

Stunned, Carla stared after Maggie as she stormed out. What were the chances of the two of them being in the same beauty salon at the same time? A million to one? But it had happened. As soon as she heard Maggie describe her husband, Carla knew instantly who she was talking about. There was only one buyer for canned soups. And only one Phil. But Maggie had spoken of him and their children with pride. She had said they were going out for an anniversary dinner that very evening.

Maggie's version of their life did not tally with the picture Phil had painted for Carla of his home life at all. He had been quite clear that the only reason he stayed at home was because of his kids. 'When our Kelly's gone, I'll be off too.' She remembered him saying that.

Her friend Sheila had warned her. They had been standing at the water cooler when Phil had passed and winked at Carla.

'You don't want to trust him,' Sheila had said. 'He tries it on with all the single women.'

Carla had just laughed. She didn't think any more about him.

But after a few drinks at the summer conference, he was all over her. All charm and smarm. He wasn't bad looking for a man of his age. He had a decent amount of hair, a twinkle in his eye, and a few funny chat-up lines. He didn't dress badly either. They had sat together, heads almost touching. He had run his finger over the back of her hand. After most of their colleagues had left the bar, Phil had sworn to her that he and his wife were as good as leading separate lives.

She had almost laughed. That was the oldest line in the book. But she had let herself fall for it, because she had wanted a bit of company and some fun. She had chosen not to think what the truth might be.

He was different from the men she had met Internet dating. They had all been such losers. Always so sorry for themselves. Or too keen to please. Or looking for a wife. Phil was none of those things. He was always up for a laugh.

Besides, she didn't want a life partner. She certainly was not going to be a threat to his marriage. No one would ever come close to her Ian. He had been everything she had ever wanted in a man. But every now and then it was nice to have someone to cheer up the odd lonely evening. She didn't care about the winks and nudges from her workmates. What did they know? As long as she wasn't harming anyone, what did it matter?

But it turned out that she was.

She knew what she had to do. 'Wait!' she called. Her only answer was the slam of the door and the wild tinkle of its bell. Snatching her hand from the manicurist, she stood up.

'I've got to talk to her. I'll be back to pay in a minute.' Without waiting for a reply, she left the two girls staring after her, open-mouthed.

She hadn't planned what she was going to say, but she had to try to put things right. Outside the shop, she looked left then right. About a hundred yards down the street, she saw Maggie leaning against a wall, bent forward as if about to faint. By the time she reached her, Carla was out of breath.

'Are you OK?' She touched Maggie's shoulder.

Maggie snapped upright at the sound of her voice, shaking off Carla's hand. 'What do you think? Of course I'm not OK.'

'There's a café here. Let me get you a coffee... a drink of water. You should sit down.'

'If I wanted to sit down, the last person I'd sit down with would be you.' Maggie's face was ashen, her eyes red-rimmed. She looked unable to move.

'Come on,' said Carla. 'You've had an awful shock. Please let me explain.' She stepped aside to let a curious passer-by go past.

'Explain!' Maggie exploded. 'Nothing you say can explain. I'm not interested.' She pulled out the tissue from her jacket pocket and blew her nose.

'Let me try. Please.' This time, when Carla touched her arm, Maggie didn't pull away. Instead, to Carla's surprise, she let herself be led into the café.

The room was crowded and hardly the ideal place for an intimate one-to-one chat, but what choice was there? As they went through the door, they walked into a din of chatter and the hiss of a coffee machine. The smell of coffee and sandwich fillings wafted round them. Most of the tables were taken but as Maggie and Carla looked around, two young women vacated one at the back of the room.

'Quick. Why don't you grab that one?' said Carla. 'I'll get us something to drink. What would you like?' She was already regretting having acted on impulse. Getting the drinks would give her a moment to think of what she was going to say.

'Black coffee. No sugar.' Maggie almost spat the order at her.

Carla watched as Maggie stepped over bags of

shopping, squeezed between chairs and round a buggy before reaching the empty table. She pulled out a chair and sat down, facing the front of the shop, looking stormy. Carla thought about doing a runner then and there. Too late. Their drinks were being passed across the counter.

She followed Maggie's route, holding the mugs high so she could see where she was going, then sat down opposite her. She put the mugs on the table, then twisted round to hang her bag over the back of her chair. She turned to face Phil's wife.

Maggie's short dark hair was still on end after the facial. It lifted away from her kind oval face. Fine wrinkles fanned out at the corner of her eyes. Her mouth was drawn in a tight line. A vein in her temple throbbed. Carla could almost see the thoughts whirring round the other woman's head. She dressed well, like her husband. A bit dowdy for Carla's taste, but each to her own.

'Before you say anything, I want you to know—' Carla began.

'Don't even try to justify yourself,' snapped Maggie. She crossed her arms over her jacket, carefully keeping her newly done nails untouched. 'I don't even know why I came in here. I should go home.'

'Perhaps because you wanted to hear me say

sorry? And I am. Truly.' Carla shivered, then remembered she had left her coat in the salon. 'And probably because you wanted to tell me what you think of me.'

Maggie raised her eyebrows, widened her eyes. 'Sorry! Do you think saying sorry will make everything all right? Just like that. Of course it won't. You're nothing but a tramp. I should have guessed the moment I saw those shoes.'

Carla was not going to be thrown by an insult like that. 'Don't be silly,' she said. 'You like them. You said so.' She pushed one of the mugs across the table.

Maggie lifted it, paused then banged it down on the table.

'Look,' Carla began before Maggie could go on. 'I don't make a habit of snaring married men.'

'You expect me to believe that?' Maggie dug into her jacket pocket. She pulled out a clean tissue and unfolded it.

'Phil told me that his marriage was as good as over.' As soon as she saw Maggie's face crumple, Carla realised that she had gone too far. 'I should never have listened, but I was lonely and I wanted to believe him. I didn't think about what I was doing. I didn't mean any harm. I would never have got involved with him if I'd known the truth was so different.'

17

'You're a liar.' Maggie squeezed the words out between blowing her nose and dabbing under her eyes.

'Look, I don't need anyone else's man. I've had the only one I want. There are plenty to be found in the dating agencies. Not that they're much cop. Phil and I just had a bit of a laugh. That's all.' Carla took a sip of her coffee, wishing she had a nip of brandy to put in it to give her strength.

'A laugh? With someone else's husband?' The coffee was bringing Maggie back to life.

A few heads turned towards the drama unfolding at the back of the café. Carla lowered her voice. 'I've told you what he said. And it was never serious.'

'You called him your boyfriend. That sounds serious to me.' The tissue was put away. Maggie's expression changed from sad and shocked to stony.

Had she called him her boyfriend? Carla thought back. Oh God, yes she had. 'What else would I call him? My lover? You wouldn't have liked that any better.'

The little colour that had returned to Maggie's face drained away. 'How long has it been going on?'

'Since the summer conference.'

A gasp. 'That long.'

'Only on and off.' And now off for good. This was more detail than was good for either of them. Carla finished her coffee. Time to go.

'I know that,' said Maggie. 'I'm not a complete idiot. We went away to his mother's for Christmas. He's been home every night, even if he has come in late.' There was a note of triumph in her voice.

Carla didn't feel it was the moment to point out that making love didn't always have to happen at bedtime. Besides, Phil had told her that his and Maggie's sex life was as good as over these days. She had believed that.

However, there was no need to rub the poor woman's nose in it any more than she had already. 'Look,' Carla said calmly. 'I don't want any of this. The last thing I want is to be the cause of someone else's marriage breaking up. I'm really sorry. If only I'd stopped to think... All I want you to know is that I'm going to put him straight as soon as I can. As far as I'm concerned, it's over.'

'And where do you think that leaves me?'

Carla was stumped for an answer.

'You think that your dumping him will make everything all right? Really?' Maggie's eyes blazed with anger.

Carla shook her head. 'Perhaps not. But what more can I do? I can't undo our conversation.' Until things went wrong, she had been enjoying their chat. It was rare to instantly hit it off with a stranger like that.

Maggie pushed her chair back and stood up. 'I'm going home now. I hope we don't meet again. And if I ever find out that you've seen him again, you'll regret it.'

'We work together, so I can't help but see him.' Carla had to point that out.

'You know exactly what I mean.' Maggie got out her purse and almost threw some change onto the table. 'For the coffee.'

'You don't have to.' She shunted the cash back towards her.

'I don't want anything from you.' Maggie began to make her way around the table. 'Not even a coffee.'

Carla got up so they stood face to face. 'I'm so sorry this happened. You have my word that our affair...' She noticed Maggie wince as she said the word. '...is over. What you do now is up to you.'

Maggie looked at her and shook her head with disgust. 'Women like you give the rest of us a bad name. Next time you want a new man, try to find one that isn't already taken.'

'I told you . . .' But it was no good. Maggie wasn't listening to her. She was marching out of the café.

Left alone, Carla looked down at her hands. Her manicure was ruined. She sighed. She needed to go back to the salon to pay and pick up her coat. She could repair the damage herself rather than sit another minute in Beauty Unlimited. What mattered now was going home and putting matters straight.

# Chapter Three

The bus dropped Maggie off at the stop at the end of their road. There was something comforting about the familiar identical red brick houses that she knew so well. This was her world. She felt safe here.

She walked towards their house remembering how excited they had been to buy it all those years ago. A home of their own. This was where they had brought up Jack and Kelly, where they had friends. She greeted old Mrs Fellows who was pottering in her front garden at number 5. She walked around a kid's bike that had been left on the pavement outside number 17. She picked up a small woollen glove and put it on the gatepost. Somebody – Alison from number 25, she thought – shouted something but Maggie didn't reply. Her sole focus was on getting through her own front door.

Her hand shook as she put her key in the lock of number 35. She shut the glass-panelled door behind her, put the key on the table on top of the post, and dropped her bag on the carpet.

'Hallo!' she called, not expecting a reply. This was a habit born from years of not knowing whether the kids were in or out. As usual she was greeted by silence. She had often thought how nice it would be to have a dog or a cat to welcome her home. Maggie had always envied the joy with which some pets greeted their owners every time they came through the door. But Phil had always said he would not have an animal in the house, so their kids had grown up without pets – not even a hamster or a goldfish.

In the kitchen, everything was as neat and tidy as she had left it. That was the thing she missed about Jack and Kelly not living there any more. Now, if she put something somewhere, it stayed there. Everything was always the same. She put the kettle on and made herself a cup of strong tea. She leaned against the white units, cradling the mug in her hands, staring out at their garden. Phil had spent so much time getting the small lawn perfect, the flowerbed just so.

That woman! Carla! To think that at first she had liked her! All those nights when she believed Phil had been staying late at work, he must have been with her. In front of her was the table that she had left laid with two wine glasses, a red rose and a candle. Their anniversary! What a joke! Beside them sat the glass trophy he had brought home at the weekend after his side won in his precious local football league. Without thinking, she picked it up and hurled it onto the tiled floor where it smashed into pieces.

The crash brought her to her senses. She didn't care about how upset Phil would be, but she did care about the mess. She got out a dustpan and brush, swept up the whole lot and dropped it into the flip-top bin, letting it snap shut.

Upstairs, she closed the bedroom curtains, shutting out the view of the street. Enough light came through them for her to see as she took off her clothes and dumped them on the pale green bedspread. She had chosen it to match the cream-and-green striped wallpaper, despite Phil thinking that the colour was too bland. Perhaps it was. She bet Carla would never have a colour like this in her house.

The shower water splashed over her while she relived the conversation with Carla. There was no doubt that Phil had been up to his old tricks. God only knew how many other women there were, whom Maggie didn't know about. At least Carla had been honest. Maggie was grateful for that. Carla had also seemed genuinely sorry.

The question was: What was Maggie going to do about it? Looking down at her body, she could see that the years had not been as kind to her as they had to some women. But she did try. She was careful what she ate. She watched what she drank. She occasionally even went to the gym.

She stepped out and towelled her hair dry. Wrapping herself in her dressing gown, she returned to the bedroom and the wardrobe. She opened both doors.

In the left half hung Phil's suits. Beside them were his white work shirts that she washed and ironed and hung so they wouldn't crease. Next to them were the coloured shirts he wore when off duty. In the top drawer of the chest of drawers were all his ties, neatly rolled, ordered by colour. There was no doubt that Phil was a dapper dresser. He was proud of his clothes.

She thought of the kitchen scissors hanging in their place on the knife rack. How easy it would be to destroy his clothes. How satisfying. She imagined herself chopping a couple of inches off every trouser leg, or cutting out the crotch from every pair. She felt the pleasure of slicing through shirt fronts or snipping off every button. She thought of his horrified reaction – and smiled.

But she would never do that. Those were the actions of a mad woman, a bunny boiler, not those of Maggie Blackburn, responsible mother of two. In any case, she could not bear to think of the waste. She would rather give his clothes to charity.

She glanced at the family photo taken at Jack and Gail's wedding. What would Phil's mum say about her darling son if she knew what he got up to? In the photo Sonia's expression was stern. But there was little love between the two of them these days. Phil left Maggie to deal with his mother. The older Sonia got, the more demanding she became and the less he wanted to do with her.

Downstairs, the front door slammed. She shut Phil's side of the wardrobe and concentrated on what to wear. Would they even go out for a meal now? She picked her favourite dress. As she put on her make-up, she could hear him moving about downstairs. She should at least look her best to confront him. She owed that to herself.

'Maggie!' Phil's voice travelled up the stairs. 'Come down. I've got something for you.'

For her! That couldn't be right. The last time he gave her an anniversary present was more than five years ago. That time, he had come home with a new steam iron for her. She gave herself a slick of coral lipstick, and stared at her reflection. What did Carla have that she didn't? The answer shrieked at her. She had energy, life, a sense of humour – that was immediately obvious. Maggie felt weary at the thought. Her eyes stung with tears again.

Phil was waiting for her at the bottom of the stairs. 'It's outside. Come and see.' He didn't even look at her before opening the front door. Her efforts were wasted as far as he was concerned. She might as well have been wearing a bin liner for all he cared. He, on the other hand, was smart in his pale grey suit and deep pink tie. With his hair slicked back like that he reminded her of David Beckham.

She followed him outside, stopping herself from saying anything about meeting Carla. Now was not the moment for a fight. Then she caught her breath. In front of her, in their parking space, was a shiny bright red car that did not belong to them.

'It's ours,' Phil said, grinning from ear to ear. 'At least I've put down the first payment.' He opened the driver's door and got in, grasping the steering wheel, wiggling the gear stick.

She saw him looking into the rear-view mirror and grinning again.

He half got out. 'You going to get in or not?' She could hear the impatience in his voice. 'I thought we could have a quick spin before we go for dinner.' From his tone it was obvious that he was not much looking forward to the meal.

What he meant was, he couldn't wait to be seen driving the car. This wasn't a present for her at all. She couldn't even drive. A sudden burst of loathing for him welled up inside her as she climbed in.

'I met someone you know today.' The words left her mouth before she had time to think.

'Oh, yeah?' He tutted as he adjusted the wing mirrors. He could not have been less interested.

'Yeah,' she echoed, as she did up her seatbelt. 'Someone from your work.'

'Mmm.' He turned the key and revved the engine, closing his eyes with bliss at the sound.

'Carla,' she said.

The car jumped forward and stalled. Phil's knuckles were white on the wheel. He turned to her. Two spots of colour burned on his cheeks. So there was no mistake. Maggie died a little inside. What now?

'Where did you meet *her*?'

'At the beauty place on the High Street. I used the voucher you gave me. I wanted to look good tonight.'

For the first time, he looked at her. His eyes halted on the nail varnish. 'Nice woman.'

'Yes. That's what I thought until she told me you were her "boyfriend".' There was a catch in her voice. Her world was falling apart and she couldn't stop it.

'Where did she get that idea, then?' His eyes shifted from Maggie to the road and back again.

'Don't pretend, Phil. I'm not a fool.' She made herself take a deep breath, but she couldn't stop the tears that were running down her cheeks. 'Why?'

'It's not what you think,' he began, raising his hand to greet a neighbour who was waving at them as he walked past. He would not want anyone to think anything was wrong. 'It was just a bit of fun.'

Wasn't that what Carla had called it?

At last he let go of the wheel. His left hand drifted past the gear stick and took hers. 'I wouldn't do anything to hurt you. I promise you that. You mean the world to me. You and the kids.'

'But this has hurt me. It's hurt me as much as it did last time.'

His eyes were shining. Was that a tear? He rubbed his cheek.

'And the kids aren't here any more.' Maggie sniffed.

'I'll give her up tomorrow, if that's what you want.'

'Of course it's what I want!' She stopped

herself from shouting but, inside her, something shifted. Was that really what she wanted? She had thought so. But now, she wondered if she had the energy to care.

After the last time, she really believed everything would be different. She had done all she knew how to make the marriage work. Her life had revolved round him for more than twenty-five years. As he had become more successful and confident, she became less so. It was as if he had drained her of the life she once had. Yet, still she had tried.

'Then that's what you'll get, Button.' He squeezed her hand.

Her heart leaped a little at the use of his pet name for her. Then she remembered. 'That's what you said before.' She pulled her hand away and sat as far from him as she could, squashed against the door.

'This time I mean it.' His eyes were dark, pleading. 'Really.'

'You said that, too.' But what would she do if they didn't make up? Where would she go?

'I do.' He leaned towards her, shrouding her in an aftershave she didn't recognise. His kiss was hardly passionate, but it was at least a kiss. That rare thing.

'Do you?' She wanted to believe him, but everything in her was telling her not to.

'I'll prove it to you, Button. I'm sorry. I've been stupid. This needn't make any difference to us. Just give me one more chance.' He sounded so ashamed. He looked at her as if she was the only girl in the world ...

She nodded. She couldn't resist that look, that wink. 'This is the very last time, Phil. I mean that, too.' And this time she did. He would not cheat on her again and get away with it.

'It's a deal. It's over. Promise.' Both his hands were on the wheel before one slid towards the key. 'And now ... shall we?'

She didn't need to reply. The evening would go ahead as planned. She would ask him more about Carla. No doubt he would justify himself some more. Afterwards they would lie on their separate sides of the bed, neither of them wanting to make the first move for their different reasons. Or maybe, this once, she would.

# Chapter Four

Carla heard the car pull up outside, the door slam, the central locking beep, and his usual double ring of her bell. She turned down the CD player. *Cabaret*. Phil hated the songs from the big West End musicals that she and Ian had loved so much. They filled her with joy as she sang along to them. And sometimes she wept. Even though she had listened to *Les Mis* a million times, 'Bring Him Home' always reduced her to a blubbering wreck. If only someone would bring Ian back to her.

She took a slug of her gin and tonic, wiggled her hips to straighten her dress, and pushed her hair behind her right ear. She was ready.

As she opened the door, Phil leaned forwards to kiss her. She turned her head just in time so his lips only grazed her cheek. He walked into the house as if he owned the place. She followed him into the living room, admiring his bum for the last time. All that football had given him a great body for a man of his age. She stopped herself right there.

'What're you having, Button?' He stood by the drinks cupboard and sent her one of his most winning smiles.

Hearing his pet name for her almost made her forget her resolve. 'G 'n' T. But I've got one. You help yourself.'

He fetched himself a beer from the fridge. When he returned, he looked more worried than she had ever seen him. The email he had sent her at work had been brief. 'We must talk. Tonight?' Of course, she had guessed at once what had happened. However, she was going to play it cool. Very cool.

'What's so urgent?' she asked. Might as well make him sweat a little, drag his agony out. 'I thought we agreed to go to the quiz at The Admiral tomorrow. Meeting twice in one week could become a habit.' She gave a little laugh.

'You must have guessed.' Phil flopped into the sofa. He leaned forward with his head in his hands.

'She told you?' Carla had been in no doubt that was exactly what Maggie would do.

There was a groan from the sofa and a nod.

'What were you thinking when you gave us both a voucher to the same beauty salon for Christmas?' After she and Maggie had gone their separate ways, that had struck Carla as the most insulting thing of all.

'I didn't think you'd go there during the week,' he replied as if the whole thing was her fault. 'And I didn't think you would speak to each other if you did.'

'Which goes to show how little you know about women.'

He perked up at that. 'Little? You're joking. Women are my special subject.' He tilted back his head as he laughed at his own joke. 'Anyway, I only bought a voucher for you. Our Kelly got the voucher for Maggie at the last minute. I hadn't got her anything, and Kelly thought her mum might like it. It was too late when I realised.' He took off his jacket and placed it over the arm of the sofa. His shirt was ironed so there were not even creases in the sleeves. 'And I never really thought she'd use it.'

So he didn't even buy his own Christmas presents for his wife. Carla shook her head. Why hadn't she thought twice before getting involved with him? She should have taken Sheila's warning to heart. But no, she always knew better. Now everything would be so awkward at work. Hadn't Maggie said he was going for a promotion? He hadn't mentioned it to her. If he took over from Mark, the trading manager, Phil would be her boss. A dreadful thought. Perhaps she should start thinking about a new job.

'So what are we going to do?' Phil got up and stood beside her at the fireplace. He took her hand, the one not clutching her gin and tonic. She raised her drink to her lips, so his kiss was deflected for a second time. He caught sight of himself in the mirror, raised a hand to slick back his hair.

'Do?' she asked, puzzled. 'I would have thought that was obvious. You and me? It's over, Phil. Surely you see that?'

He could not have been more stunned if she had punched him in the stomach. He took a step back as if to help him focus on her better. 'Over?' he asked as shock raced across his face. 'What on earth? But why?'

'You told me your marriage was over,' she reminded him. 'You said that you and she were like strangers. You told me only the kids kept you together. I can't believe I let myself fall for all that.'

She turned and straightened the photo of her husband that she kept on the mantelpiece. Ian beamed at her from the saddle of his Harley Davidson. That was the last holiday they had together, roaring round Cornwall, staying at pubs, going to that bikers' meet, being bikers together. Crazy times.

Phil caught her arm. 'You mean the world to me, you know that. This needn't make any difference to us.'

His words had a funny second-hand feel about them. There was something in his voice that made Carla feel he had said them before. She looked around at the jewel-green walls of her living room, the pictures, the bright tapestry cushions she had sewn herself, the wonky clay sculptures made by her nephew and nieces, the bits and pieces she'd collected over the years. The snow globe collection that she'd started as a joke now took up the length of the window sill. Her knitting sat on the arm of the chair begging to be taken up again. This was her nest. She was happy here with only Bumble her tabby cat for company. 'Of course it makes a difference,' she said firmly. 'I liked Maggie. She doesn't deserve that.'

'She won't know, Button.' His smile reminded her of a shark. He had definitely overdone the tooth whitener. He sat down again, messing up the purple throw over the back of the sofa. 'Come and sit here.' He patted the cushion beside him.

Instead, she took the comfy chair between him and the fireplace.

'She won't know,' he repeated. 'I'll make sure of that.' His eyes were dark, insistent. 'Really. Nothing between us needs to change. That's what I came here to say.'

'Is that what you've told her?' Carla could not believe his nerve.

He had the grace to look shame-faced. But only for a moment. 'I'm sorry. I've been stupid. Just give me one more chance.' He sounded so repentant. He looked at her as if she was the only girl in the world . . .

But Carla was not going to make the same mistake again. What was more, she could be as firm as him. 'I'm sorry too. But I'm not the kind of woman who does that to someone's wife.'

'Who are you kidding? Deep down, you knew perfectly well what the situation was and chose to go along with it. Nothing's changed.'

She remembered the hurt on Maggie's face. 'Everything's changed. I should never have got involved with you.'

He snorted. 'Bit late for that now, isn't it?'

If she could have run a knitting needle right through him without being had up for murder, she would have. Instead she had to make do with a glare. 'It's never too late, Phil. Time you learned that.'

'You're not serious?' His astonishment at being

dumped was almost comical. His mouth opened and shut. He held out his hands to her in appeal. 'Come on. We're having a good time. We enjoy each other.'

'We were,' she corrected him. 'Not any more. I think you'd better finish your beer and go.'

'What about work?' A flash of anger entered his voice.

'What about it? We'll behave as if nothing's happened.' As she might have predicted, relief crept across his face.

'You won't go to HR, to Personnel then?'

'And say what?' Who did he think she was? 'Of course not.'

A dreamy look crossed Phil's face. She knew he was thinking about Jackie Sinclair, the new head of HR and conveniently single. The man was shameless. Jackie had only recently joined the company and had already made quite an impression. Phil had been unable to stop talking about how much he rated her. He wouldn't ... would he? Carla had a nasty feeling she was about to find out – unless she changed her mind.

At the door, he turned to her. 'Don't suppose you'd fancy a run in the new motor? I could drop you somewhere.'

Beyond him she saw a gleaming red Vauxhall

parked too close to her little Fiat. 'Nice,' she said. 'But I don't think so.'

Stroking his tie, he winked at her. 'Remember that time in the old one? In the cemetery? You liked that.'

She almost smiled at the memory. She had never thought she'd have sex in a car again. And then she met Phil. But he had known where to go – a place where no one could see – and one thing had led to another...

'Come on,' he said. 'What harm's a little spin going to do?'

She had to hand it to him. He didn't give up easily. 'We–ell...' She hesitated. They were already at her gate.

He seized the moment and unlocked the car. He jumped into the driver's seat and leaned across to open the passenger door. 'Hop in. You won't regret it.'

With the memory of what happened in the cemetery pulling at her, she climbed in.

As he revved the engine, a smug expression stole across his face. Then he glanced in the mirror and gave a little nod as if to say, 'I knew you wouldn't be able to resist me in the end.'

She immediately swung her legs out of the car. 'What are you doing?'

'What does it look like? Bye, Phil. See you at

work.' With that, she slammed the door so hard the car shook. Having given herself that small pleasure she went indoors, wondering whether she should tell Maggie that she had done what she had promised.

# Chapter Five

Maggie was ironing Phil's shirts when the phone rang. She stopped what she was doing and took the phone to the kitchen table.

Since their anniversary, Phil had been trying to make an effort. He was still working hard for his promotion. He often stayed late at the office but he always came home in a good mood. They had even had sex a couple of times in the same week. That was something they had not done for years. She had even heard him whistling in the garden.

In return, Maggie was trying not to hold the affair against Phil. But she had a long way to go before she could forgive him completely. For now she was doing her best to repair the damage he had done to their marriage. She got on with her daily tasks as usual. Those little gestures should add up. However, forgiveness was hard when she could not get Carla out of her mind. How could she when Phil was at work with the woman every day?

When she heard Carla's voice, Maggie almost hung up. But something kept her listening.

Carla came straight to the point. 'I know you won't want to talk to me.'

'You're right. I don't.'

'Would you meet me? I'd like to clear the air between us.'

Carla's invitation caught her on the hop. Maggie's surprise was doubled when she heard herself agreeing. But she couldn't deny her curiosity. Phil had assured her the affair was over. She wanted to make absolutely sure that Carla knew that too.

When the day came, Maggie took care to dress carefully. She paired a flowery skirt with a pale turquoise T-shirt. She painted her nails with the pearliest of varnishes and made herself up using a new foundation she had read about in a women's magazine.

Carla lived on the other side of town – two bus rides away. Maggie found the small Victorian cottage tucked between two terraces quite easily. The window boxes contained a riot of petunias. The door was painted a warm green. On either side of it were two tubs of something that looked like red grass. She paused for a moment before going down the short path. Was this a mistake?

But she had come all this way. She would not let herself chicken out now.

Carla flung open the door and welcomed her in. 'I'm glad you came.' But Maggie could tell she was nervous too from the non-stop chatter as Carla led her through to the raspberry and vanilla-coloured kitchen.

Maggie's eyes were on stalks. Carla's style was nothing like her own. Even so, Maggie loved the colours, the chaos, the warmth of the other woman's home. Ornaments were crowded on every surface. Pictures and photos hung on every brightly coloured wall. Carla put on the kettle and fished out the tea caddy from a cupboard that was nothing like Maggie's tidy ones at home. The stripy mugs hung from hooks underneath a shelf.

They went outside to sit in the small garden that was bright with flowers.

'Can I tempt you?' Carla picked up the plate of biscuits and held it out.

Maggie shook her head. She had always been careful with what she ate since Phil had become so critical of her weight. But he obviously had not minded Carla's. What was that about?

'Oh, treat yourself.' Carla helped herself to a flapjack. 'Life's too short to sweat about the small stuff. And these are good. I made them myself.'

Despite the tension in the air, Maggie found herself smiling. She reached out for one. Carla was right. The flapjacks were good.

'But I asked you over for a reason.' Carla sat a little straighter and touched the glossy red beads round her neck. 'I wanted to assure you that I finished with Phil the day after we met.'

'You mean he finished with you.' Maggie gave a short laugh and helped herself to another biscuit.

'Er, no. That's not what I meant.' Carla looked startled.

'Well, whoever said what ... I'm glad it's over. And I'm pleased that you asked me here.' Maggie looked around her. A pair of coal tits pecked at the bird feeder. A tabby cat sprawled in the sun. Somewhere a dove cooed.

'You've made it up with Phil, then?' Carla sounded concerned.

'Oh yes. He said it was just a bit of fun.' Maggie reached out to Carla. 'I'm sorry. I hope that's not too hurtful to hear.' In fact, she hoped it was just the tiniest bit hurtful.

Carla shook her head and cradled her mug in her hands. 'Not at all. I said that too, if you remember.'

'He said he wouldn't do anything to hurt me and that I meant the world to him.'

Carla frowned but Maggie didn't want to stop to ask why. She wanted Carla to understand that everything was fine now. Her marriage was back on track. It was almost as if Carla never existed. 'Yes,' she went on. 'He said, "I'll do what you want, Button." That's what he's called me ever since we met,' she explained, feeling a warm glow at the memory. 'What's the matter?'

Carla's frown had deepened. She had put down her mug and was staring at her. 'He calls you Button?' she asked very slowly, as if she was trying to work something out.

'Yes.' Maggie laughed. 'Silly, really but – well, it's—'

'But that's what he called me,' Carla interrupted. 'Button!' She said the word with disgust.

'That can't be right ...' Button was Maggie's special name – hers – chosen by Phil because of her tiny nose. But as she looked at Carla, Maggie realised she had to be telling the truth.

The other woman's eyes were shut. A redness on her chest had risen over her neck and up to her cheeks. Carla was taking a deep breath as if she was thinking. Her fingers tapped against each other. Her fuchsia-pink nails glinted in the sun. When her eyes opened, she seemed to have made a decision. Maggie felt suddenly nervous. She didn't want to hear what Carla was about to say. She pushed her chair back, ready to stand up and leave.

Carla held out her hand, indicating Maggie should stay where she was. She cleared her throat, obviously finding it difficult to say what she wanted. 'Look, I don't want to tell you this but I think you should know something.'

Maggie's heart was hammering against her ribs.

Carla took her hand. 'Those things he said to you . . . He said exactly the same to me. The exact same words. "You mean the world to me. This needn't make any difference to us. I've been stupid. Just give me a chance." Any of them sound familiar?' She stopped. 'I'm so sorry.'

Maggie felt as if bit by bit she was cracking up inside. She swallowed. 'He didn't dump you?' she asked quietly, staring down at her wedding ring.

Carla gave a little shake of her head. 'I'm afraid not. I had to spell out that I wanted nothing more to do with him and his lies. He thought we could carry on as if nothing had happened.'

Maggie began to cry. How could she have been so easily taken in again? This time her marriage was over. But what would the children think? And his mother? What would their friends think? What would she do? She felt Carla's grip

46

tighten on her hand. She squeezed back as if clinging to a life raft.

'He's been lying to us both all along. And now he's probably lying to Jackie too. Or whoever else he has his eye on.'

'Jackie?' Maggie choked out. Through the tears she could see the sympathy on Carla's face.

'The new woman in HR. He's in and out of her office like a yo-yo these days.'

'Not the promotion?' Maggie clutched at her last hope.

'Maybe that, too.' But Carla sounded doubtful. 'I'm so sorry. Would a drink help?' She didn't wait for an answer but went inside. She came out minutes later with two glasses of rosé.

Maggie never drank before seven in the evening. She had never drunk pink wine in her life. But what did any of that matter now? What had she got to lose? She raised the glass to her lips.

For a while, they sat without talking. Maggie tried to think, but her head was spinning. As soon as she managed to fix on one thing, something else darted in and took its place.

Carla sat in thoughtful silence. Eventually, she spoke. 'It seems to me you could use a friend right now. And I think I could help you.'

'I can't go home and confront him all over again. He'll only lie to me and talk me round.'

Maggie despaired. 'But what else can I do? If we split up, where will I go?' She pictured Kelly's tiny student room with its single bed. As for Jack? Well, Gail would never want Maggie in the house for longer than a night at the most. And she would never impose on her friends.

'Maybe together, we can be cleverer than that?' Carla suggested, cautious at first. 'There's strength in numbers. Or so they say.'

'How do you mean?' Only hours earlier, the idea of the two of them doing anything together would have been unthinkable to Maggie. But who else was there to turn to? She couldn't tell the children. She didn't want to tell her friends. And she certainly didn't want anyone at school to know. The gossip would spread like wildfire fanned by the mothers at the school gate. She had seen that happen before. No, she had to sort it out for herself first.

'Perhaps we can play with him a bit? Make him sweat while you work out what you want to do.' Carla leaned towards Maggie. 'Seems to me that you've spent the last twenty-five years looking after your family and putting yourself second. You've got to put yourself at the top of the heap again. Life's for living, not for feeling sorry for yourself. And it's certainly not for putting up with cheating husbands.'

'"Play with him"? How?' Even though what Carla said made a kind of sense, how could Maggie change after so long? Breaking the habits of a lifetime seemed an impossible task. Carla was asking her become a different person. There had to be another way through this.

But why should Phil be allowed to get away with what he had done? Carla was right. Since school, Maggie had devoted herself to making Phil's life as comfortable as possible. And this was how he repaid her.

'How?' she repeated.

'I'm not sure yet.' Carla held up a finger. 'But two minds work better than one. So let's have a think.' She returned inside to get the bottle of wine.

Maggie stared at Carla's retreating back with some surprise. Against all odds, she had found in this woman someone she could trust. More than that, she might even have found a friend.

As afternoon gave way to evening, they began to make a plan.

By the time Maggie had to go home to get Phil's dinner, she was ready.

# Chapter Six

The early morning was Carla's favourite time of day. She got up, made herself breakfast with a coffee of heart-starting strength, and sat with her tabby, Bumble on her knee. This was when she planned the day ahead.

Today was slightly different, however. Her mind was still on the previous afternoon and her chat with Maggie. Would Maggie wake up still as determined to get even with Phil? Or would her courage have deserted her over night?

When they weren't cooking up their plan, they had talked about things other than Phil. Carla was truly interested in Maggie's work and the teachers and kids she worked with. She had told Maggie about Ian, and how supportive his family had been to her. They had touched on Maggie's two children and Carla's fondness for her nephew and nieces. Gradually they had relaxed, sometimes even laughing and interrupting each other.

Button! Phil had even given them the same pet name. How could he? Carla punched her fist on the arm of her chair. A little cloud of dust rose in the air. Bumble opened an eye in surprise then closed it again. His purring grew louder as she tickled between his shoulder blades.

'What shall I do?' Carla asked the tom-cat. 'What shall *we* do? I won't let Phil get away with this.'

Bumble just purred louder still.

Meeting Maggie again had confirmed to Carla that her first instincts had been right. On the surface they might be quite different, but they had more than enough in common to be friends. Maggie might be more reserved, but Carla guessed she was ready to come out of her shell. And Carla could help her. Perhaps she would even suggest they go shopping together. She had plenty of ideas how Maggie's outfits might be jazzed up. A splash of colour was the answer to so many things. She tapped her pink nails on the table as she thought.

Since Ian died, she had thrown herself into her career. Being appointed a buyer at Plums was a step on her career ladder. She was proud of that. She did not want to give up her job. But neither did she want to report to Phil. She had too much pride for that. She sighed. Jobs were hard to come by these days.

Her brain began to work faster. At last she had

a good idea. Of course! Perhaps she could find another job somewhere else in the company? Her skills would be good for other work. Perhaps she did not have to be tied to buying. When she got to the office she would make an appointment to discuss things with HR.

Luckily, Carla was able to fix a meeting for three o'clock. The morning ticked past slowly. She reviewed her budget, then checked the stock levels in the new ketchup promotion. Running out would be a disaster when the promotion was going so well.

She was aware of Phil at his desk on the other side of the room. He was dressed as sharply as usual in a navy-blue suit, white shirt, polished shoes. Whenever she looked up, he was staring towards her. Each time she looked away. Once he even winked at her. What was his problem? Had he really not got the message?

At last the clock ticked round to five to three. Carla went to the Ladies where she tidied her hair and touched up her make-up. She made sure she was looking her most professional.

Her knock on the door was met by a brisk 'Come in.'

Jackie Sinclair came out from behind her desk. Her curly brown hair surrounded a delicate face.

Her neat dark dress was teamed with leopard-skin shoes that Carla could kill for. A pair of reading glasses swung in her hand. Carla forced the thought of Phil seducing Jackie to the back of her mind. That did not concern her now. What mattered was that, as head of HR, Jackie was the one person who could help her. Once Carla had sat down and cups of tea were placed in front of them, she began to explain her wish to change jobs.

Jackie listened intently, her eyes never leaving Carla's face. She sat forward, her elbows on the desk. Her hands were pressed together, her fingers just touching the tip of her nose. When Carla stopped speaking, Jackie leaned back in her chair, turning it from side to side.

'Are you absolutely sure about this?'

'I'm sure it's time for something new.' Nothing would make Carla admit the real reason she needed a change.

'But your job performance assessments...' Jackie nodded towards her computer screen. 'They're so positive.' She paused. 'You know Mark's leaving?'

Carla nodded.

'Of course, I've been talking to people about who could take over from him as trading manager. We were wondering whether you might be interested.'

A sudden sense of warmth and well-being flooded through Carla. 'Me?'

'Yes. I was going to talk to you but you beat me to it. Unless your mind's made up, I'd like to encourage you to apply.' Jackie waited for Carla's reaction.

'But I thought Phil . . .' Carla stopped as the vision of a delicious revenge came into her mind.

'Nothing's been decided.' Jackie peered over her glasses. 'We want to talk to everyone who's interested in the job. Are you telling me you're not?'

'Not at all.' Carla back-pedalled fast. 'No, I'd love to have a chat about it. I didn't think that was even a possibility.'

'Good.' Jackie smiled warmly. 'I'll let you know when we're interviewing. That should be within the next couple of weeks. And if you don't get it, then we'll think again.'

The meeting was over.

On her way back to her desk, Carla passed Phil at the water cooler. He tucked his hand under her elbow and steered her behind a filing cabinet. 'What were you doing with Jackie?' he whispered, sounding anxious. Was he worried she might have reported him for harassment? She hoped so.

'Absolutely nothing to do with you, Phil.' She pulled her arm away from him. 'I might be changing jobs, that's all.'

'You're not going after Mark's?' He stared at her as if it was the daftest idea he had ever heard. 'They've virtually told me the job's mine *if* that's what you're wondering.'

'I'm not.' She looked away, loathing the arrogant glint in his eye. 'You're way out of your league with her, aren't you Phil?'

His teeth gleamed as he grinned. 'Nothing to do with you, darling. Sure you haven't changed your mind in that area? It's not too late.'

'I'm completely sure, thanks.' She left him standing there. But that short talk had been enough to put steel into her soul. Back at her desk, she took out her phone and sent a quick text.

Need to shop for special occasion. Fancy coming? Was thinking after work. Tonight? Cx

She didn't have to wait long for a reply.

Love to. Phil playing football. Need to get out of house. Thanks Mx

When Carla arrived at Hobley's department store – 'the world of shopping at your fingertips'

55

– Maggie was already there. They kissed each other on the cheek. Just one slightly cautious kiss.

'So what's this special occasion?' Maggie asked as they rode the escalators to the second floor, elbowed by late-night shoppers.

'I've got an interview for the trading manager job that's going. You know the one Phil's going after? Well, they're seeing other people too and they suggested I put my name forward.' As she spoke, Carla realised just how much she wanted the job. 'I've got to make an impression.'

'But what about Phil? He's waited for this for so long.'

So Maggie's courage was failing her just as Carla had feared. She went on the attack.

'What about him? What about me? I can't turn this chance down. You do see that, don't you?' Maggie must understand that Carla had to grab what had been offered to her.

'I suppose so.' But Maggie was quiet as they reached the women's fashion floor.

'Remember what he's done.' Carla couldn't bear the idea that Maggie might sink back into her rotten marriage. Like every woman, she deserved more than that. 'Remember what we said last night? You can't go back now. He's not going to change.'

'I know. It's just hard after so long. I need to keep reminding myself.' Maggie had lost the confidence of the previous day.

'It's bound to be hard at first but you will get through this you know.'

Once in women's fashion, Carla was in her element. She picked out a cross-over dress in a green-and-orange hummingbird print and held it out. 'This would really suit you.'

Doubt was written all over Maggie's face. But Carla was not going to take no for an answer. 'Before you say anything, just try it on. And trust me.'

Together, they made quick work of the rails, picking out the clothes they liked. Carla made sure the pastel colours chosen by Maggie went straight back where they came from. 'You told me your wardrobe was too quiet. It's time for a change.'

Eventually, carrying heaps of clothes, they took next door changing rooms. Carla was proved right. The dresses she had chosen for Maggie looked wonderful on her.

'You see what a difference a bit of colour makes,' Carla said. 'They bring you to life. Much better than those neutral shades you love so much. I'm going to get you out of your comfort zone if it kills me.'

'But I always...' Maggie stopped. She spent a long time in front of the mirror gazing at her reflection, turning back and forth.

Meanwhile Carla had found the perfect dress for the interview – a cornflower blue with long sleeves. 'What do you think? I'll wear it with my white jacket.'

'Perfect. If you're dressing to impress, that should do it.' Maggie was smiling at their reflections in the mirror. 'You know what? I do like this hummingbird dress, even though I don't look like me at all. God knows what the family will say.' She could imagine Phil and his mum clucking with disapproval.

'Forget them for once. What they say doesn't matter. You look fantastic! They'll see that. If *you* like it and feel comfortable, buy it. And then, let's get a drink. Have you got time?'

Maggie checked her watch. 'Why not?' She was flushed with the success of their trip. 'Phil can heat up his own meatballs.'

They both laughed as if that was the funniest joke they had ever heard.

In a nearby bar, they found an empty table. Still excited by their shopping trip, Maggie bought them a couple of glasses of wine. 'You're good for me, you know,' she said as she sat down.

'Glad you think so. Here's to us!' Carla raised her glass. 'May the best women win!'

They clinked glasses. Carla opened the crisps. Plain salted.

'I haven't said anything to Phil,' Maggie said. 'He went out in our "anniversary present" last night. His latest toy.' She shook her head.

'Maybe we should do something to that car,' suggested Carla. 'Hit him where it hurts.'

Maggie laughed. 'It would do that all right. But what? I couldn't damage it, if that's what you're thinking.'

Carla thought for a moment. 'You could park it a couple of roads away and pretend that it's been stolen. Let him sweat for a day or two and then return it.'

'Great idea. The only problem is I can't drive. And anyway he'd just call the police.'

'You can't drive! You're joking!' Carla coughed as her drink went down the wrong way.

Maggie shook her head. 'Nope. I never really needed to. I wish I'd learned now, of course. That's why him pretending the car is a present for both of us is so hurtful.'

'But it's not too late. Why don't you learn now? Then at least you could drive the thing.'

'He'd hate that.' The flicker of a smile crossed Maggie's lips. 'He's always been the driver.'

'All the more reason.' Carla was struck by the mystery of other people's marriages. What one woman would put up with, another would fight against. 'Why not? You said the school holidays were dragging by.'

Maggie looked at Carla over her glass. Her eyes shone. 'You know what? I think I just might.'

'Have you got his credit card details?' Carla's wink said everything. 'He needn't know immediately.'

'I pay the bills.' Maggie grinned. 'He needn't know at all.'

# Chapter Seven

'Something smells good.' Phil breezed into the kitchen. Late again.

'I thought we'd have chilli.' Maggie stirred the pot so the aroma of tomato, garlic and spices drifted up under their noses. 'Good day at the office?'

'Very.' He gave a secretive little smile. Grabbing a beer from the fridge, he opened the door into the garden. 'Still think I should have made this decking a bit wider.'

'Aren't you going to tell me about it?' Maggie was finding it easier and easier to act as if nothing had changed between them. As Carla had told her: it was all a question of getting into the right mind-set. And she was getting there. At first the idea of Phil and her splitting up seemed impossible. How would she cope? But she was beginning to think that there might be life outside their marriage.

Until she was sure, she had decided to do nothing. As she came up behind him she found herself checking for tell-tale signs of lipstick or for the hint of an unfamiliar perfume. Nothing.

'Oh, not much to say really.' He stared outside, as if he was thinking of something else. That same smile broadened. 'Got a first interview with HR for the trading manager job first thing tomorrow.'

'HR?' Maggie's stomach flipped. She could not help wondering about Jackie after Carla had mentioned her. Could he really have moved on to someone else already? That was fast work by anyone's standards. Although Carla had also said she couldn't believe Jackie would look twice at Phil. 'She's a nice woman. One of us.' For a second Maggie had felt insulted on his behalf, and on her own. Then she remembered how Phil always rose to a challenge.

'Yep. I'm going for that job. Remember?' Sometimes Phil talked to her as if she was incapable of remembering anything. 'Think I'll go up and change.' As he walked past her, he undid his collar. There was a small bruise on his neck, just under his ear. But if not Jackie, then who?

Maggie had just enough time to dish up the chilli into two large bowls. Into one of them, she slid a small pile of finely chopped chilli and garlic. Tomorrow Jackie from HR would remember her meeting with Maggie's husband.

She and Phil barely spoke for the rest of the evening. She found it hard to know what to say. Her head was teeming with thoughts about how best to play things. They sat across the kitchen table from one another. Phil ate about five mouthfuls of chilli before sweat began beading on his forehead. 'This is much hotter than usual,' he muttered, pouring himself a third glass of water.

'I don't think so.' Maggie took another forkful. 'It's the same recipe.'

To Phil, finishing a hot curry was a mark of manliness. It was one of the demands of a good evening out with the lads. However, he refused a second helping. After blowing his nose, he went to shut himself in the living room with a football match on TV. He didn't ask Maggie if there was anything she would like to watch. Instead, she threw the rest of the chilli into the bin and cleared up after him as usual.

Maggie was knocked backwards when she put her head round the living room door. The smell! The garlic must be oozing through every one of his pores. She couldn't help smiling for a moment. He would be in a perfect state for his interview in the morning.

But what about the night ahead? Maggie pictured herself tucked up next to him in bed.

She would have to endure that smell all night. Worse still, she could hear the snoring and the farting (always the result of a good chilli) that would go with it.

Revenge might be sweet, but she would suffer too. She would have to wait for another day and another chance. She sighed. This was only the beginning.

The next day Carla was laughing when she phoned. 'The garlic! My God! But there was something else, wasn't there? He went out to buy a new shirt at lunchtime.'

'I couldn't resist dabbing a little milk in the armpits, just in case,' Maggie admitted. 'I wanted to be sure that Jackie wouldn't forget him.'

'Judging by her face when he left her office, she won't. She went straight back into her office and opened all the windows.'

'I'm feeling a bit guilty now.' All day Maggie had worried that, however unfaithful Phil was, he didn't really deserve this. Perhaps it would be fairer to have it out with him one last time. Except that she was not going to do that again. She would not risk being won over. She had turned a corner in her life.

'Don't waste your time.' Carla was as firm and encouraging as Maggie knew she would be. 'Just remember what he's done. This is pay-back. But if you want to stop...'

'No,' she said, remembering how he had lied to her. 'No, I don't. Not yet.'

'See you at Zumba on Thursday then.' Carla had coaxed a very reluctant Maggie to come to her dance class. To Maggie's surprise, after half an hour of embarrassment, she had actually begun to enjoy it. She was even looking forward to the next one.

When Phil arrived home that evening he was thrilled to have got through his first interview. He had come in, flung his milk-stinking shirt into the wash basket. 'You need to get some different washing powder,' was all he said.

Maggie realised then that he would never imagine that she might find out what he was up to with the women in the office. He had got away with it for so long. Nor would he dream that she would have the nerve to try to screw things up for him. He would soon find out the truth.

The following weekend, Phil was off to a football match with the lads. It was a shame he hadn't checked his season ticket holder for the ticket before he left. Maggie had spotted the ticket peeping out from under Phil's chair in the living room. It had fallen there as he slipped the holder into his pocket. Somehow she hadn't said anything. With her foot, she edged it a little further under the chair. When Phil arrived at the ground, he would not be admitted. He would try phoning Maggie but her phone would be switched off. The landline would ring and ring, but she wouldn't be at home as she usually was. Instead she would be sprawled on Carla's sofa with a big tub of salted popcorn, a box of Toffetts and a pile of DVDs. After *Zoolander* and *Bridesmaids*, she would go home to face the music.

'What bad luck,' she sympathised. 'It must have fallen out somewhere.'

Red-faced with fury and frustration, Phil pulled the holder out of his pocket. 'How could it possibly? This has been tucked into the living room mirror ever since the last match.'

She took it from him. 'Look at this.' The stitching had come undone along one side. He hadn't noticed. Why would he? Maggie's job was to notice and mend anything that had come apart. She still didn't tell him where he could find the ticket. Wasn't it better to let him find it for himself? However long it took.

*

A new week began. As soon as Phil had left for work on Monday, Maggie sat by the front window of the living room, waiting. At ten o'clock on the dot, a car pulled up behind Phil's red baby. On its roof was a sign: 'Arnie's Driving School'. Out stepped the driving instructor. He was a man in his forties, a bit paunchy but pleasant-looking with thick hair and neat in his jeans and trainers.

Maggie opened the door before he reached it.

'Mrs Blackburn?' His smile was friendly. 'I'm Gus from Arnie's. I guess you're expecting me.'

'I am. Actually I'm a bit nervous.' He didn't need to know that this was the first time she had taken such a step without Phil's encouragement. 'But excited, too,' she added.

'Just as it should be.' He led the way back to the black Nissan and opened the driver's door for her.

'Already? But I've never ...' She stopped herself. This was the new Maggie doing this. Just get in, she told herself. And she did.

Sitting in the small car with a stranger felt oddly intimate. As Gus showed her how to adjust the mirror she noticed a third of his right ring finger was missing.

'Car door,' he explained when he saw her looking at it. 'A nervous pupil. Now, don't worry. First I'll show you the controls. Once we've done that, I'll take us somewhere you can drive without damaging anything.'

'What? Today?' Her stomach flipped over.

'Yup. There's no point hanging about. You'll probably pick it up quicker than you're expecting.' As he explained how the car worked, Maggie felt an overwhelming sense of her own power, her own potential. She was going to drive. Phil had always claimed women made terrible drivers. She would show him. Following Gus's instructions, she slipped the gear stick into first and then back into neutral. Not so hard. Now second.

Two hours later, she was worn out. They had driven to a nearby square. She had gripped the wheel as they lurched down the road. In the end she had begun to get the hang of it and her fears began to fade. Gus drove off, saying he would be back at the same time the next day.

From inside the house, Maggie stared at the shiny red car outside. If only she could move it somewhere as Carla had suggested. But she could at least sit in it and imagine herself driving. Phil had left the keys on the key rack in the hall. She took them and headed to the car. What harm could she do? Phil would never know.

She put the key in the ignition without turning it on. She checked the mirrors, adjusting the rear-view one slightly. Wiggling the gear stick she pictured herself driving away for ever. She would put her foot down and escape to a new life without Phil. She switched on the radio. Radio 2 blared out into the small space. She switched it off. In the glove compartment she found his CDs. She slipped in Michael Bublé and closed her eyes as his voice swelled around her. Phil's taste in music always surprised her. Her hand returned to the gear stick, shifting it through the gears as she imagined herself living by the sea, in a cottage, with a new man, with a dog of her own – a black spaniel. She did up her seat belt and reached for the key. She could run the engine and pretend...

With her eyes closed, she turned the key. BANG! The engine stalled. Her eyes opened immediately. What had Gus said about leaving the car in neutral? She looked down – it was in third. The car had jumped forward only to be stopped by the white Ford Mondeo in front. Oh God! Mike Bird would make such a fuss when he saw the damage to his car. As for Phil...

Maggie got out, her legs like jelly.

'What happened?' Anne Carter was leaving number 37 and came to have a look. They stood together staring at the point where the two cars had bumped. 'I thought you couldn't drive.'

'I can't,' wailed Maggie.

'Shall I reverse Phil's for you?'

'Would you?' Maggie was pathetically grateful.

When the cars were parted, Phil's dented bumper and Mike's smashed rear light were all too obvious. The thought of the trouble ahead made Maggie's heart sink.

However, back in the house, she began to see the funny side. She and Carla had wanted to get at Phil through his car. She had done that by accident. She began making supper and waited for Phil's return. To pass the time, she painted her nails a cool peony pink. Finally he came through the door.

'What the hell happened to my car?' he shouted without even saying 'hallo'.

*My* car. Not *our* car. Maggie steeled herself.

'I just wanted to see what it was like in the driving seat,' she said. 'I'm really sorry. I'll pay for the damage.'

'Damn right you will. "Just wanted to see ..." ' He put on a child's voice to mimic her. 'For God's sake! What are you? Twelve years old? That's a brand new car. I haven't even paid for it yet and you – the one who's too stupid to drive – manage to crash it. Sometimes I wonder whether you've got a brain in your head at all ...'

On he went. On and on. Insults rained down around her.

Maggie stopped listening, tuned herself out. She might be many things, but stupid was not one of them. And she didn't deserve to be spoken to this way. Not ever.

At last, her heart hardened.

# Chapter Eight

On the Sunday before the final round of job interviews, Phil was at the pub watching some football match. Carla and Maggie wondered whether the game was really a cover. Maggie had told Carla about the bruise on his neck. They decided there must be another woman in Phil's life already. If not Jackie, then someone else.

'Mind you, I wonder whether he suspects me of being up to something,' Maggie had joked. 'I'm going out more often, and I've started leaving him ready meals instead of cooking.'

'And, let's face it, you look a million dollars,' Carla had reminded her. 'Isn't that one of the sure signs of an affair?'

'Judging by Phil – I'd guess so. But, let's face it, he only notices what he wants to. It would never cross his mind that I'd do anything like that.'

The truth was that Maggie had bloomed. She certainly didn't look like a down-trodden wife any more. Her brighter clothes had worked a treat. With Carla's encouragement, she had had her hair re-styled and streaked. She was looking more confident, like a woman who had taken charge of her life.

She had been finding out about Access courses and talking about training to be a primary school teacher. If that wasn't possible, perhaps she might become a teaching assistant. The secret driving lessons had been going well, too. Carla had even let Maggie drive her car. Though they decided not to risk their friendship by trying that again. Carla would leave that side of things to Gus. Maggie seemed to enjoy her lessons with him.

Together they chose Carla's killer outfit for her next interview: a yellow jacket with a grey skirt and camisole. She had been back to Beauty Unlimited and had her nails painted a tawny red. 'Professional, not tarty at all,' Maggie said. 'That's the sort of colour I'll go for next time.'

Jackie had told Carla that they were down to the final three candidates for the job who were Phil, Carla and Jim, the home-baking buyer. Jim went about his job in his usual modest, efficient way. Phil behaved as if he was already in charge. Carla was quite sure that he had no idea that she was in the running.

At quarter to eleven the next morning, Carla was waiting outside the room where the interviews were being held. She was fifteen minutes early so she would have time to prepare herself without being rushed. She went through what she wanted to say. She knew exactly how she wanted to present herself – reliable, able and loyal to the company. She wanted to stay with Plums if she could.

But she would have to beat the others. Phil might be a love rat but he did his job well. He was on top of his budget and had brought some very successful new brands to Plums' range of soups. The customers liked him too – an essential part of the business. Jim was less flashy, but he was excellent at making deals and had a good head for figures. Carla knew she shouldn't underestimate him.

Then she reminded herself. 'You're good too, Carla Malone. You've got similar strengths. You deserve this as much as they do.'

The door of the meeting room opened. Phil came out looking horribly smug. Then he noticed her.

'What are you doing here?'

'Same as you, I guess.' She longed to prick his bubble of self-confidence.

'You're not really going for the trading manager post?' His tone was one of total disbelief. 'I understood my interview was just a formality. I don't want to crush your hopes but ... it may only be a matter of time until you're reporting to me.'

Definitely time to change the conversation. She knew just where to take it. 'Pink's not usually your colour is it?'

Phil looked down at his shirt. He pulled the slightly too short sleeve of his suit towards his wrist. 'Maggie managed to put all my white shirts in the wash with my red sweater last night.' He couldn't have made her sound more useless. 'I only found out this morning. After years of doing our washing, she managed to screw up for one of the most important days of my life.'

'This is the twenty-first century, Phil. Plenty of men do their own washing now.'

'Not me! And...' he added, 'she took my best suits to the dry cleaner. I couldn't believe it!'

Carla hid her smile. She knew just how long it had taken Maggie to find that red sweater – a Christmas present to Phil from his mum. She also knew what had happened to many of his suits. Maggie had described to her the pleasure of the charity shop worker who had accepted them. If Phil kept his eyes open on the way home, he might see them in the window. Both she and Maggie knew that messing with his clothes might mess with his head. But there was no way they would threaten his promotion chances.

They had drawn the line at that. The promotion board would see beyond the colour of his shirt. But once the interviews were over, they did have one last plan.

'Carla?' Jackie was at the door. 'Would you like to come in?'

'Best of luck,' said Phil, and winked.

She took a deep breath. 'Thanks.' Better to be gracious than to hit him.

When she left the room an hour later, her head was swimming. She had faced a board of three members of management, including Jackie. They had quizzed her about the job she had. They had asked her how she would manage the job she wanted. She thought she had given the best answers she could. But the detail of what she had said had already blurred in her mind.

On her way back to her desk she passed Phil on his way to the test kitchens. 'Off to try some new soups,' he said, as if she might be interested. 'How did you get on?'

'Oh, quite well, I think,' she replied, not wanting to let him think she had any doubts.

'Not too well, I hope.' He laughed. 'Don't want my chances ruined!' He clearly didn't think for a moment that they would be. 'They said they'd let us know by the end of next week. God knows why it has to take so long.'

She shrugged her shoulders. 'Actually Phil, I…'

But he was a man in a hurry. 'Sorry, Carla. Got to get on. Places to go. People to see. You know how it is.'

After an afternoon on the phone to several clients, planning her own store visits and supplier briefs, Carla was exhausted. When she got home, she changed gratefully into a long, loose, linen dress and took her tea and her mobile into the garden. Her cat Bumble followed her to sprawl on a sun-warmed patch of the patio. She cut dead flowers from a few rose bushes, pulled out a weed or two and thought about what she might put in the gap where a lavender bush had died. Gardening always relaxed her, but she had one thing left to do. Once it was done, she could make supper.

She picked up her mobile and called the number. She listened to it ringing. Just as she was giving up, she was connected.

'Carla?' He sounded tense.

'Yes. Is this a bad time?' She bent over to tickle Bumble's tummy. The cat stretched full length and rolled onto his back.

'No, not bad.' She heard a door being shut at his end. 'Better if Maggie doesn't hear me though.'

Same old Phil.

'I've been thinking since I saw you this morning,' she said.

Silence.

'We're obviously going to go on working together so maybe I was a little hasty.'

'What do you mean?'

'I mean that perhaps we could give it another go?' She watched Bumble tense as a ginger cat came over the wall.

'And Maggie?'

'Like you said. She wouldn't have to know. I was wondering about a weekend away in ten days time. Once this job's been decided. We can celebrate whichever one of us has got it. What do you say?'

'Away?' He sounded unsure.

He was going to be difficult. Perhaps she had left this too late.

'Yes, away. One night in a B&B by the sea. You won't regret it.' She put on a husky drawl.

'Is that a promise?'

Ah! She'd hooked him. Now all she had to do was reel him in, like a fish.

'Oh yes, it's a promise. I need to make things up to you.'

'I don't know if I could get away. Things haven't been easy here recently.'

'Just one night...' She could almost hear his brain whirring. 'Couldn't you tell a tiny white lie? I'll make it worth your while.' She didn't know how to make a night in a B&B sound more tempting. 'Remember what fun we used to have?'

'Saturday night? It'll be hard.'

Just one more tug of the line and she would have him landed, home and dry.

'Well, if you don't want to...'

'I do, I do. OK, yes then. You book it and I'll be there.'

Got him!

'Good. It's been way too long. I hope you haven't forgotten everything I taught you.'

'How could I?' He gave a dirty little laugh. 'And what about the things I taught you?'

She laughed back – a sexy giggle. 'But no one at work must suspect a thing.'

'They won't. You have my word.' For once she believed him. He wouldn't want anything to get in the way of his promotion. Rather in the same way she didn't want anything to get in the way of hers.

# Chapter Nine

Maggie was determined to make the weekend one Phil would not forget. She had planned it down to the last detail. All she had to do was to break the news to him. She waited until after a good supper. A set of new white shirts was hung up upstairs. The car's bumper had been repaired and paid for by her. The season ticket had been found. All was well in the world. Or so Phil thought.

He had finished watching his DVD of *Planet Earth* when she joined him in the living room. He looked surprised when she sat down. Recently, she had been staying as far away from him as she could.

'Next weekend,' she said. 'We're not doing anything so ...' She saw something flicker in his eyes. She moved on quickly. 'So I've asked your mother over.'

'You've done what?' He sat up straight, glaring at her.

She carried on, despite his clenched jaw. She could see the tiny movements he made as he ground his teeth. 'She's coming on Saturday. She was thrilled.' Actually Sonia had been as surprised as Phil obviously was, but there was no need to tell him that.

'But she came at Christmas,' Phil said defensively. Indeed she did. She had spoilt the whole occasion by being difficult and tetchy. The food had not been to her taste. The children (as she still saw them) had made the wrong career choices. The TV was too loud, or too quiet. Phil should have known she needed her walking stick. Maggie had forgotten her electric blanket again. On and on she went.

'Exactly. Seven months ago. When she gave you the red sweater that you loved.'

'That you shrunk.' He still hadn't forgiven her. 'She'll go mad if she finds out.'

'Accidents happen.' Maggie pictured happily the tiny red felt-like sweater with one sleeve longer than the other. That and the pleasantly pink shirts that had come out of the boil wash. 'We don't see her enough,' she said.

In fact they saw his mother more than enough. Sonia didn't hide her belief that Phil could have done better than Maggie. But Maggie wanted this to be a weekend that Phil would remember – if for all the wrong reasons.

'We see her plenty. You know what she's like.

Anyway I won't be here.' His gaze swerved past Maggie to the posy of flowers she had put on the mantelpiece.

But Maggie was not going to let him get out of this. 'There's nothing in your diary. I checked. She'll expect you to be here and to drive her home. You'll just have to change whatever you've planned.'

Their argument was brief. For once Maggie didn't back down in the face of Phil's refusal. Eventually, surprised by her firmness and with very bad grace, Phil agreed to see what he could do.

Maggie laid the red summer dress on the bed. She straightened the skirt so it would not crease. On the floor was a new pair of strappy high-heeled sandals.

She leaned forward, checking her face in the mirror. The make-up session Carla had insisted they took in the House of Fraser had been embarrassing. Maggie had hated being made up in front of a crowd of staring shoppers. But there was no doubt she looked younger, thanks to the new methods she had learned and the products Carla had made her buy.

Carla had arrived in Maggie's life at exactly the right time – even if in exactly the wrong way. As

Maggie came to terms with the truth about Phil, Carla's outlook on life had begun to rub off on her. Maggie saw at last how ground down she had been by her home life and years of habit. Carla had shown her that anyone could enjoy life to the full, but only if they chose to.

Maggie didn't have to be school secretary for ever. There were other careers she could go for. She thought of Gus, her driving instructor. After two or three lessons, she had begun to see him quite differently. With his sense of humour and calm in the face of danger, he was quite a sexy man. There was something about his missing finger ... Who would have thought that she would ever look at a man other than Phil in that way? She was pleased to find that side of her hadn't shrivelled up and died.

Fresh out of the shower, Maggie dropped the towel on the floor and dressed quickly. She sang along to the iPod – 'I'm Gonna Wash that Man Right Outta My Hair' from *South Pacific*. Corny, but oh how appropriate. She had almost picked up Carla's enthusiasm for musicals – but not quite. However, some of those songs perfectly matched her mood at the moment.

She ran a finger over the bottles of nail varnish she had recently bought. Pale, pretty shell pink? No. Deep raspberry red? No. Dark dahlia. No, not quite right. She picked up a gleaming blood red. Yes, yes. That was perfect. Maggie glanced at her watch. She had just enough time. She picked up the bottle, unscrewed the top and began to paint her nails.

When they were dry, she checked herself in the mirror again, took the scarf and draped it round her shoulders. Beside the pale orange, green and pink, the red dress lost some of its impact. When she opened the bedroom door, she heard voices downstairs.

Sonia had arrived while Maggie was waiting for her nails to dry. She was complaining to Phil about the journey. Maggie could hear the tension in his voice when he replied. They both looked up when she came into the room.

'When did you get that?' said Phil, his stare making it clear he didn't like her outfit one bit. 'And the nails – what's possessed you?'

'I like it,' said Maggie. 'What do you think Sonia?' She braced herself.

Sonia was looking her up and down, an unfamiliar look on her face. 'I've never seen you in anything like that before, but the colour suits you. The nails, too. I'm surprised.'

Had Maggie just died and gone to heaven? Compliments from Sonia were rare and all the more precious because of it.

Phil gave one of his snorts. He shook his head as if he had never heard of anything so silly.

She ignored him. 'I thought we might have lunch in the garden.' She stood at the window and looked up at the sky. 'It's a beautiful day.'

'Good idea. I'll get the cushions from the shed.' Phil stood up. 'By the way, I may have to go out this evening, Mum. I thought I could cancel an outing with the lads, but they've begged me to go with them.'

Sonia sniffed loudly. She would have to face a mini cab smelling of pine air freshener or stale cigarette smoke.

Maggie glared at Phil. She would make sure he drove Sonia when the time came.

'I'm sorry.' There was a brief flash of that quiet smile of his. For once he helped Maggie prepare the outside table. Was he feeling guilty? As guilt had never troubled him before, she thought it unlikely.

Just as they were about to sit down, the doorbell rang. Phil was sorting out a more comfortable cushion for Sonia, so Maggie went to answer it.

'Who was that?' asked Phil when she came back.

'A friend I met recently. I've asked her to join us for lunch. You don't mind, Sonia?' She took off the scarf and put it over the back of her chair. 'She'll be out in a second.'

'Who?' asked Phil.

'You'll see.' Maggie smiled at him.

Losing interest, Phil went back to making his mother comfortable.

A moment later, Carla stepped into the garden. She was dressed, like Maggie, in red. Hers was a crimson that perfectly matched the gleaming red of her fingernails.

Maggie would have paid good money to see the expression on Phil's face. His eyes widened and his mouth dropped open as he looked from one of them to the other. But with Sonia there, he could say nothing. All part of the plan. And of course Sonia had no idea what was going on.

'Phil!' Carla greeted him with a peck on the cheek. 'I work with Phil,' she told Sonia. 'You must be his mother.'

'I thought you were going away this weekend.' Phil looked as if he had seen a ghost.

'Cancelled,' she said with a laugh. 'No. I never really wanted to go anyway. Instead I thought I'd come round to share my news. I was called yesterday and offered a new job as trading manager. I've accepted of course.'

Phil groped for the side of the table to steady himself, then sat down.

If Maggie didn't know the truth, she might have felt sorry for him. But he deserved this. She had no doubt there would be other chances for him. Other women too. He had been abusing her trust for years. He had taken her for granted, never thought what she might be feeling. He lived without a thought for anyone but himself.

Maggie had allowed him to do that without seeing what she was doing. She had been so taken up with bringing up Kelly and Jack. She had thought Phil was too. She had believed he was working so hard for his family. But now the children were gone. Revenge had been a long time coming.

'We must celebrate then,' said Sonia, clearly hoping that someone new might ease the family tension. 'Why don't you get the bottle of Cava I brought?'

Looking as if he'd been slapped hard, Phil went inside. Carla and Maggie grinned at each other.

'How did you two meet?' asked Sonia as Phil came out, clutching a bottle and glasses.

Phil busied himself with the drinks. His shoulders were tense and the back of his neck was a telling shade of pink.

'We met having our nails done,' Maggie said. 'We were both given a voucher for a new place on the High Street. Phil gave me mine for Christmas.'

'And my ex gave me mine,' added Carla.

Phil coughed as if something was stuck in his throat.

'We got chatting and the more we got to know about each other...' Carla stopped to take a glass of bubbly from Phil. 'Well, the more we found we had in common, I suppose.'

There was a splutter from Phil as his drink went down the wrong way.

'How nice,' said Sonia, as if she didn't think it was particularly nice at all. She raised her glass. 'Here's to your new job. Did you have to see off much competition?'

'Thanks,' said Carla, raising her glass in reply. 'No, nothing I couldn't handle.'

The lunch was simple but good. Even Sonia seemed happy with the grilled salmon and salad followed by fruit salad and cream. Phil, however, hardly touched what was on his plate.

'He's had the appetite of a bird since he was a child,' Sonia said to Phil's obvious embarrassment.

Whenever he thought his mother wasn't looking, he would stare at Maggie and Carla, confusion and anger doing a tango across his face. To avoid any unwanted set-to, the two friends made very sure that neither of them was left alone with him. This was their afternoon and they wanted to enjoy it. Carla threw herself into the fun. Phil was the only one not to laugh at her jokes. Even Sonia warmed to her, telling her proud stories of her son's achievements. Phil looked as if he wanted to crawl into a hole and hide.

Eventually as lunch gave way to tea, Maggie could not resist asking, 'What time do you have to go, Phil?'

'I'm not going anywhere any more, as you well know.'

Sonia looked puzzled. 'But I thought...'

'I had a text. One of the lads is ill.' His mouth was pulled into a grim line of fury as he lied for Sonia's benefit.

'So you can take me home after all?' For a moment, Maggie saw how much that meant to Sonia. For once, her heart went out to her mother-in-law. Sonia was just a lonely old woman who wanted the company and love of her son. That wasn't much to ask. It was such a shame that she had been landed with an only child who had always been too selfish to give her what she wanted. No wonder she was bitter.

Just before they left, Maggie followed Phil into the kitchen. Alone at last.

He turned on her, his face blazing with rage. 'What the...'

'Don't say anything, Phil. I know how you tried to carry on your affair with Carla. You even called her "Button" too.'

That stopped him in his tracks. Phil hung his head to stare at the floor. His foot traced the joins of the tiles.

Maggie went on. 'I also know now that she would never have been the last. I know you, Phil. You can't help yourself. It's been a long time coming to a head, but we can't go on like this.'

He tried to interrupt her, but this time she would not let him.

'When you get back, I'll have packed a case and I won't be here. Carla has cleared out her spare room for me. I'm going to stay there until I sort myself out.'

'You can't do this. You won't be able to manage.' He looked up, his eyes filled with fear and panic.

'You know what, Phil? I think I'll manage very well. You may be the one in trouble when you haven't got an unpaid skivvy and cook any more. There are too many broken promises between us. Don't you see? I can't trust you. The kids don't need me any more. I want a crack at living my own life, and Carla has helped me realise that I can do that before it's too late. If you're stuck, you've got my mobile number.'

'But Carla ... of all people ...' Phil was lost for words.

'Phil!' Sonia's voice echoed through the house. 'Are you ready?'

He gave Maggie a long hard look, as if seeing her for the first time. She could tell that he knew there was no point arguing. This was the end of the line. Then he turned away. 'Better not keep her waiting. Just coming,' he yelled, before turning back to Maggie. 'Go if you must. But you'll be home before you know where you are.'

'I don't think so,' she said to the back of his head as he left the room.

Maggie went upstairs to finish her packing. She heard the car doors slam and Phil drive off. She took a long last look at the bedroom. Her heart thudded.

Taking a deep breath and giving herself no time for second thoughts, she walked downstairs to where Carla was waiting. They should go. Gus was arriving at Carla's at seven o'clock to take her out for a drink. The first, she hoped, of many.

Amy's Diary — Maureen Lee
Beyond the Bounty — Tony Parsons
Bloody Valentine — James Patterson
Blackout — Emily Barr
Chickenfeed — Minette Walters
Cleanskin — Val McDermid
The Cleverness of Ladies — Alexander McCall Smith
Clouded Vision — Linwood Barclay
A Cool Head — Ian Rankin
A Cruel Fate — Lindsey Davis
The Dare — John Boyne
Dead Man Talking — Roddy Doyle
Doctor Who: Code of the Krillitanes — Justin Richards
Doctor Who: Magic of the Angels — Jacqueline Rayner
Doctor Who: Revenge of the Judoon — Terrance Dicks
Doctor Who: The Silurian Gift — Mike Tucker
Doctor Who: The Sontaran Games — Jacqueline Rayner
A Dreadful Murder — Minette Walters
A Dream Come True — Maureen Lee
The Escape — Lynda La Plante
Follow Me — Sheila O'Flanagan
Four Warned — Jeffrey Archer
Full House — Maeve Binchy
Get the Life You Really Want — James Caan
The Grey Man — Andy McNab
Hello Mum — Bernardine Evaristo

| | |
|---|---|
| Hidden | Barbara Taylor Bradford |
| How to Change Your Life in 7 Steps | John Bird |
| Humble Pie | Gordon Ramsay |
| Jack and Jill | Lucy Cavendish |
| Kung Fu Trip | Benjamin Zephaniah |
| Last Night Another Soldier | Andy McNab |
| Life's New Hurdles | Colin Jackson |
| Life's Too Short | Val McDermid, Editor |
| The Little One | Lynda La Plante |
| Love is Blind | Kathy Lette |
| Men at Work | Mike Gayle |
| Money Magic | Alvin Hall |
| One Good Turn | Chris Ryan |
| Out of the Dark | Adèle Geras |
| Paris for One | Jojo Moyes |
| The Perfect Holiday | Cathy Kelly |
| The Perfect Murder | Peter James |
| Pictures Or It Didn't Happen | Sophie Hannah |
| Quantum of Tweed: The Man with the Nissan Micra | Conn Iggulden |
| Red for Revenge | Fanny Blake |
| Rules for Dating a Romantic Hero | Harriet Evans |
| A Sea Change | Veronica Henry |
| Star Sullivan | Maeve Binchy |
| Street Cat Bob | James Bowen |
| The 10 Keys to Success | John Bird |
| Tackling Life | Charlie Oatway |
| Today Everything Changes | Andy McNab |
| Traitors of the Tower | Alison Weir |
| Trouble on the Heath | Terry Jones |
| Twenty Tales from the War Zone | John Simpson |
| We Won the Lottery | Danny Buckland |
| Wrong Time, Wrong Place | Simon Kernick |

# Discover the pleasure of reading with Galaxy®

Curled up on the sofa,
Sunday morning in pyjamas,
just before bed,
in the bath or
on the way to work?

**Wherever, whenever,
you can escape**
with a good book!

**So go on...**
indulge yourself with
a good read and the
**smooth taste of**
Galaxy® chocolate.

Proudly supports

Quick Reads are brilliant short new books written by bestselling writers to help people discover the joys of reading for pleasure.

Find out more at **www.quickreads.org.uk**

 @Quick_Reads    TheQuickReads

We would like to thank all our funders:

**LOTTERY FUNDED**

We would also like to thank all our partners in the Quick Reads project for their help and support: NIACE, unionlearn, National Book Tokens, The Reading Agency, National Literacy Trust, Welsh Books Council, The Big Plus Scotland, DELNI, NALA

At Quick Reads, World Book Day and World Book Night we want to encourage everyone in the UK and Ireland to read more and discover the joy of books.

World Book Day is on 5 March 2015
Find out more at **www.worldbookday.com**

World Book Night is on 23 April 2015
Find out more at **www.worldbooknight.org**

Start a new chapter

# Out of the Dark

## Adèle Geras

Rob Stone comes back from the horrors of the First
World War with a ruined face and a broken heart.
Lonely, unable to forget the things he has seen, and
haunted by the ghost of his dead captain, all that
Rob has left is a picture of the captain's family.
Rob sets out to find them, hoping that by giving
them the picture, he can bring peace to the
captain's ghost – and to his own troubled heart.

**Quercus**

Start a new chapter

# Red for Revenge

## Fanny Blake

Two women, one man: code red for revenge...

Maggie is married with two grown-up children.
Her twenty-five year-old marriage
to Phil has lost its sparkle.

Carla is widowed. She understands life is short
so she lives it to the full. But is her new romance
all that it seems?

When the two women meet in the beauty salon,
they soon find they have more in common
than the colour of their nails.

The discovery that they are sharing the same
man is shocking. How will Phil be taught
a lesson or two he won't forget?

**Orion**

Start a new chapter

# Dead Man Talking

## Roddy Doyle

Pat had been best friends with Joe Murphy
since they were kids. But five years ago
they had a fight. A big one, and they haven't
spoken since – till the day before Joe's funeral.
*What*? On the day before his funeral
Joe would be dead, wouldn't he?
Yes, he would...

**Jonathan Cape**

Start a new chapter

# Paris for One

## Jojo Moyes

Nell is twenty-six and has never been to Paris.
She has never even been on a weekend away with
her boyfriend. Everyone knows she is just
not the adventurous type.

But, when her boyfriend doesn't turn up
for their romantic mini-break, Nell has the
chance to prove everyone wrong.

Alone in Paris, Nell meets the mysterious moped
riding Fabien and his group of care free friends.

Could this turn out to be the most
adventurous weekend of her life?

**Michael Joseph**

**Quick Reads**

*Start a new chapter*

# Street Cat Bob

## James Bowen

When James Bowen found an injured street cat
in the hallway of his sheltered housing, he had no
idea just how much his life was about to change.
James had been living on the streets of London
and the last thing he needed was a pet.

Yet James couldn't resist the clever tom cat,
whom he quickly named Bob. Soon the two were
best friends, and their funny and sometimes dangerous
adventures would change both their lives, slowly
healing the scars of each other's troubled pasts.

Street Cat Bob is a moving and uplifting story
that will touch the heart of anyone who reads it.

**Hodder & Stoughton**

Start a new chapter

# Pictures Or It Didn't Happen

## Sophie Hannah

**Would you trust a complete stranger?**

After Chloe and her daughter Freya are rescued from disaster by a man who seems too good to be true, Chloe decides she must find him to thank him. But instead of meeting her knight in shining armour, she comes across a woman called Nadine Caspian who warns her to stay well away from him. The man is dangerous, Nadine claims, and a compulsive liar.

Chloe knows that the sensible choice would be to walk away, but she is too curious. What could Nadine have meant? And can Chloe find out the truth without putting herself and her daughter in danger?

Hodder & Stoughton

# Why not start a reading group?

If you have enjoyed this book, why not share your next Quick Read with friends, colleagues, or neighbours.

A reading group is a great way to get the most out of a book and is easy to arrange. All you need is a group of people, a place to meet and a date and time that works for everyone.

Use the first meeting to decide which book to read first and how the group will operate. Conversation doesn't have to stick rigidly to the book. Here are some suggested themes for discussions:

- How important was the plot?

- What messages are in the book?

- Discuss the characters – were they believable and could you relate to them?

- How important was the setting to the story?

- Are the themes timeless?

- Personal reactions – what did you like or not like about the book?

There is a free toolkit with lots of ideas to help you run a Quick Reads reading group at **www.quickreads.org.uk**

Share your experiences of your group on Twitter 🐦 @Quick_Reads

For more ideas, offers and groups to join visit Reading Groups for Everyone at **www.readingagency.org.uk/readinggroups**

Other resources

# Enjoy this book?

Find out about all the others at **www.quickreads.org.uk**

For Quick Reads audio clips as well as videos
and ideas to help you enjoy reading visit the
BBC's Skillswise website **www.bbc.co.uk/quickreads**

Join the Reading Agency's Six Book Challenge at
**www.readingagency.org.uk/sixbookchallenge**

Find more books for new readers at
**www.newisland.ie**
**www.barringtonstoke.co.uk**

Barrington Stoke

Free courses to develop your skills are available in your
local area. To find out more phone 0800 100 900.

For more information on developing your skills
in Scotland visit **www.thebigplus.com**

Want to read more? Join your local library. You can borrow
books for free and take part in inspiring reading activities.